Cast Your Vote

Sara Mitchell

illustrated by Donna McKenna

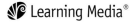 Learning Media®

Contents

1. Power to the People

Usually when a teacher says "Listen up – I've got a great project to tell you about," I start thinking about what I'll do over the weekend. But I have Ms. Cassidy this year, and everyone says she's cool. So when she said she had an announcement, I decided to give her a chance.

"You all know that the state elections are coming up," she began. (It wasn't such a great start, but it did get more interesting.) "I thought this would be a good time to hold our own election for a class president. He or she will represent our class on the Student Council. I'll be taking nominations over the next few days."

Sofia Pacheco started waving her hand in the air like a drowning person trying to signal a lifeguard. We'd only been in fourth grade for a few weeks, but I could guess what Sofia was going to ask.

"Ms. Cassidy, can a person nominate herself for class president?"

Ms. Cassidy gave a little smile. "Yes, Sofia. As long as someone is happy to second the nomination."

Sofia's hand bounced back up. "I'd like to nominate myself. I'm sure Jennifer will second it," she said confidently. Jennifer nodded shyly. She was Sofia's best friend.

Blake, my best friend, rolled his eyes. "I don't know why we're bothering with an election," he mumbled. "Everyone will vote for Sofia – she'll tell them they have to!"

2. The Candidates Are …

At lunchtime, everyone was talking about the election. "David and Sean are thinking about running for class president, too," said Sally.

"They're both so serious!" said Blake. "We need someone who's fun." Blake liked having fun. He was always clowning around and thinking of new things to do. That was why he was my best friend.

"I agree," I said, scrunching up my juice box and throwing it high over Blake's head. The juice box smacked into the trash can. "Yes! Juan the Unbeatable makes another basket, folks!" I said in my best sports commentator voice. "The question is, can he do it again?"

I was so involved with my superhero fantasy, it took me a few seconds to notice that Sally and Blake had huge grins on their faces. "You're our man, Juan," said Blake. "I'm going to nominate you for class president."

"And I'm going to second it," said Sally. She took a bite of her apple, and I knew it was no use arguing. The subject was closed.

I wasn't so sure I wanted to run for class president, but the next day, I saw Sofia handing out rosettes that said "Vote for Sofia." She looked so smug. That's what helped me make up my mind.

"Great," said Blake when I told him I was committed. "Now we just have to make sure you win!"

Later, I wished I'd kept my mouth shut.

"All right," said Ms. Cassidy that afternoon. She was standing in front of the whiteboard with her hands behind her back. Whenever she stood like that, we knew she meant business. "The election speeches will be on Friday. This is when the candidates will talk about their platforms."

I couldn't concentrate on what Ms. Cassidy said next. The words "speeches" and "platforms" were ringing in my ears. I hated giving speeches, and I didn't have a clue about platforms. I thought that the class president should try to make school a fair place for everyone – and fun – but how was I going to make that happen? Blake was the one who had all the good ideas – not me. I tried to let him know that I wasn't happy, but he was too busy listening to Ms. Cassidy. At least that was a good sign.

3. Cookie Time

Riding home on the bus, I started freaking out. Blake gave me some advice. "Forget about the speech for now," he said. "What you need is a platform that will make you stand out. What are you good at?"

"Nothing much …," I said. "Playing basketball and baking cookies," I added glumly. Then I had a brilliant idea. "Hey, I could make cookies for the class. We could put a message on them that says 'Vote for Juan.'"

"That's a cool idea," said Blake. "They'll be much better than Sofia's rosettes. Hey – I know." Blake was on a roll. "Don't say 'Vote for Juan.' Say 'Juan the Unbeatable.'"

I nodded, a big smile on my face, but Blake wasn't finished yet. "Figure out some campaign promises while you're baking. I'll do some newspaper research. It might give us some ideas." He got off at his stop, already lost in thought.

The next day, Sally helped me hand out the cookies. They went down brilliantly with everyone – everyone except Sofia, of course. Sally said Sofia threw her cookie right into the trash. She didn't even taste it.

I didn't care because the cookies gave us a great chance to find out what everyone thought the class president should do. Some people were dreaming. Tammy said she'd vote for me if I could make the burgers in the cafeteria bigger, and Sam wanted a skate park. Other kids had better ideas, like having a parents' night. Now I just had to decide what my platform would be.

4. The Cookie Crumbles

When my idea for a platform finally hit me, it was like the time I was smacked in the face with a basketball. I didn't see it coming, but when it hit, I couldn't understand how I'd missed it. I scribbled a note to Blake and Sally calling an emergency campaign meeting at lunchtime.

Before I could tell them my great idea, Sally burst out with news of her own. "Sofia is telling everyone that there was a cockroach in her cookie. She says you were trying to poison her!" I stared at Sally, too shocked to speak – but there was more. "Sean's worried that he's going to be next, so he's pulled out of the election. But the worst thing of all – David says you gave out cookies to bribe people. He's going to complain to Ms. Cassidy."

By the time Sally had finished, her voice was a shrill squeak. Blake looked dumbstruck. I felt sick. "What am I going to do?" I moaned, my idea forgotten. "My reputation's ruined. Ms. Cassidy will probably disqualify me!"

"There's only one thing you can do," said Blake. "Win the election fair and square and prove them all wrong!"

The rest of the week flew past like a rollercoaster. Ms. Cassidy didn't disqualify me. She just gave a big speech to the whole class about election rules. We learned that bribery – or anything that even looks like bribery – is a big no-no. Another big no-no is lying about another candidate (especially if that lie is about creepy-crawlies in cookies).

After Ms. Cassidy's talk, things settled down a little – although Sean wouldn't change his mind about running for president. While we worked on our speeches, the rest of the class made a ballot box and ballots. The election was between Sofia, David, and me …

5. Campaign Promises

Suddenly, it was Friday – speech day. My stomach felt like a cement mixer. Luckily, David was first up. He made a big deal about the class president needing to be serious and responsible. Sofia was next. Her friends began cheering before she'd even started to speak. They soon stopped when they heard what she had to say.

"When I'm class president, I'll set up a reward system for people who hand their homework in on time." Sofia's cheesy smile was so big it was bouncing off the walls. Everyone knew that Sofia always got her homework done on time – and she got good grades. She sat down looking pleased.

Then it was my turn … and it was weird. As soon as I got up to speak, I didn't feel nervous anymore. I felt excited. Suddenly, the election wasn't about keeping Sofia from becoming president. It wasn't about being Juan the Unbeatable, either. It sounds kind of corny, but it was about helping the kids in my class.

"I guess you know that I'm not the most serious person around," I began. Blake smiled and gave me a thumbs-up. "I don't get the best grades, either, but I want to make a promise that I think is great. The reason it's great is that everyone in the class can take part."

I looked around, and all the faces suddenly made me feel uncertain. I glanced at Ms. Cassidy, and she gave me a smile and a nod. Maybe she knew I was onto something. So I took a deep breath and sailed on.

"If I were class president, I'd start a class newspaper. Then everyone would have a voice. There could be articles on anything you wanted, and if you didn't want to write for the newspaper, you could draw cartoons or help to put the paper together or something. We could all work as a team." That was all I had to say.

I went back to my desk, blushing furiously. It was over. I was so relieved, I didn't even hear everyone clapping. I just wanted to go home and do nothing except enjoy knowing that it was all over. Now, it was the voters' turn.

6. Hot off the Press

After the adrenalin rush of the speeches, the actual election was no big deal. Ms. Cassidy was the election officer, which meant she was in charge of counting the votes. David got five votes, but the big news was that Sofia only got three. When she heard, she tried to pretend that she didn't care – even though we all knew she did.

The rest of the votes went to me. I couldn't believe it. It was true that I'd called myself Juan the Unbeatable, but I hadn't really believed it. I never dreamed that the kids would vote for me instead of Sofia. I hoped that she'd get over it – I didn't want her as my enemy. Suddenly, I had my first great idea as class president.

"Ms. Cassidy," I said, raising my hand. "As class president, I think we should have an election to choose an editor for our paper."

"What a great idea, Juan," said Ms. Cassidy.

"I'd like to nominate Blake," I added with a wicked grin.

"I'll second that," said Sally.

In the front row, Sofia's arm waved madly in the air.

Democracy

The United States is a democracy. This means that the people can vote for the government and have a say in who leads their country. The students in this story held a class election that was democratic. They each voted for who they wanted to be class president.

The ancient Greeks first talked about democracy more than fifteen hundred years ago. Of course, the powerful rulers at the time didn't like this idea. They were used to making all of the decisions, and they prevented democracy from happening.

By the 1500s, people began to hear about democracy and to challenge their rulers. Over the next 350 years, many kings and queens were replaced by elected leaders. This wasn't always a peaceful process. The Revolutionary War happened because the American people decided that they wanted a democratic system.

DIGGING DEEPER

Political Talk

Before an *election* is held, people are usually *nominated* to run for a position. Sometimes the nomination needs to be *seconded* by another person. Blake nominated Juan for class president, and Sally seconded him. People who have been nominated are called *candidates*, and they call each other *opponents*.

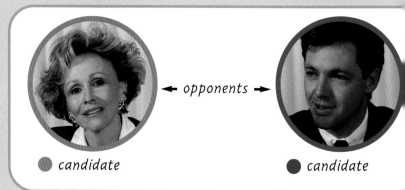

←— *opponents* —→

candidate　　　　　*candidate*

Candidates usually have a *party* that supports them. The party organizes a *campaign* to convince people to vote for their candidate. The campaign may include public speeches and advertisements. The candidate has a *platform*, which is a list of things that he or she promises to do if elected. Juan's campaign promise was to publish a class newspaper.

A campaign that makes another candidate look bad is called a *smear campaign*. Sofia's claim that she found a cockroach in her cookie is an example of this.

party members

On election day, people vote for the candidate that they prefer. They write their choice on a *ballot*, which is put into a ballot box. The *returning officer* counts the votes and announces the winner. If somebody wins by a large margin, as Juan did, it's called a *landslide* victory.

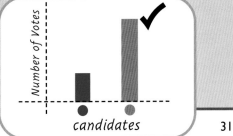

31

Votes for All

In a democracy, everyone over a certain age gets to say who they want to become the leader of their town, state, or country. The democratic process usually ensures that we have leaders who are popular and have the support of the majority. It also helps to ensure that all politicians are chosen by the people. Without this process, a leader might just seize power — not caring whether they have the support of the people.

The democratic process works best when everyone has their say. However, in many countries, voting isn't compulsory. As a result, not everyone who *can* vote *does* vote. Some people might not understand the election process or have the information they need to make an informed choice. Other people aren't interested in voting. In many elections, less than half of all the eligible voters turn up to vote.